HERE COMES TOD!

Five enchanting read-aloud stories about the eventful days of a very lively little boy.

Philippa Pearce is one of the most popular children's book authors. Her titles include the modern classics *Minnow on the Say, A Dog So Small* and *Tom's Midnight Garden,* for which she was awarded the Carnegie Medal in 1959. She also won the 1978 Whitbread Children's Book Award for *The Battle of Bubble and Squeak*. She lives in a village in Cambridgeshire, where many of her books are set.

Adrian Gon trained as a graphic designer in Italy. Now a freelance illustrator, his books include the Walker titles *Kid Kibble* (by Diana Hendry) and *Good Night, Sleep Tight* (by Penelope Lively).

Some other titles to read aloud

HERE COMES TOD!

by
PHILIPPA PEARCE

Illustrations by
Adriano Gon

WALKER BOOKS
AND SUBSIDIARIES
LONDON • BOSTON • SYDNEY

To my daughter
and the editor of this book

First published 1992 by
Walker Books Ltd, 87 Vauxhall Walk
London SE11 5HJ

This edition published 1993

4 6 8 10 9 7 5

Printed in England

British Library Cataloguing in Publication Data
A catalogue record for this book
is available from the British Library.
ISBN 0-7445-3089-X

CONTENTS

"I've a parcel for you, Tod."

TOD AND THE SURPRISES

There was a little boy called Tod who lived with his mother and his father and his teddy bear; and his granny lived not very far away.

One morning, after Tod's mother had gone off to work, there was a ring on the front doorbell. Tod ran to the door and lifted the flap of the letter-box to see who was there. At first, all he saw was a pair of trousers. Then the man outside stooped down to look at Tod looking at him. They recognized each other. Tod called back to his father in the kitchen, "It's the postman." And the postman said, "I've a parcel for you, Tod. It's too big to go through the letter-box."

So Tod opened the door and took the parcel in, and ran back to his father with it. "I wonder what it is," he said. "And I wonder who's sent it to me."

"I know who's sent it," said his father, "because I recognize the handwriting on the outside. It's from your granny. Though why she should post something to you, when she could easily come and hand it over to you herself, I can't think."

"I can think," said Tod. "I've always wanted a surprise to come to me by the postman; and Granny promised she'd send me something. Granny always keeps her promises."

"Your granny spoils you," said Tod's father. "Aren't you going to open your parcel?"

"Yes," said Tod. He was feeling the parcel gently between his hands. "But I like not knowing what the surprise is. I think it may be a helicopter. Granny knows I want a helicopter."

Tod began undoing the parcel. His father helped him untie the string, and then he opened the wrapping paper. Inside there was something knitted in red wool.

"Oh," said Tod. "Not a helicopter."

"No," said his father. "It's a lovely red jumper that your granny's knitted for you. Try it on, Tod."

"Now?" said Tod.

"Of course," said his father.

So Tod tried on the jumper, and it fitted. Then his father pointed out that something blue had been knitted on the front. "Why!" exclaimed his father. "It's a T – a big blue T for Tod!"

Tod stared down his front at the big blue T for Tod. His father said, "When you wear your new jumper, Tod, everyone will know who you are. 'Here comes Tod!' they'll say. 'It must be Tod because he's got a big blue T for Tod on the front of his red jumper.'"

"Yes," said Tod slowly. "Yes. They will, won't they?" He began to smile to himself. He patted the blue T on his front. "I like this jumper."

Tod telephoned his granny to thank her for his new jumper. Then Tod's father spoke to his granny. "It's such a beautiful jumper," he said. "I hope you didn't have to work too hard at making it. How long did it take you?"

"Not long," said Tod's granny. "It took me just about a week."

"Anyway," said Tod's father, "Tod loves it. He wants to wear it every day. But he'll have to wear something else when we need to wash it."

"That's a pity," said Tod's granny. "I hadn't thought of that difficulty."

*Tod telephoned his granny to thank her
for his new jumper.*

Then they all took turns at saying goodbye to Tod's granny – Tod said it, and then Tod's father, and even Tod's teddy bear, who happened to be in the kitchen at the time.

Just about a week later there was another ring on the front doorbell. Tod went to the door again and came back with another parcel from the postman. His mother was cleaning the kitchen, because his father had gone to work – he worked on Mondays, Tuesdays and Thursdays. Tod held out the parcel to his mother: "Is it from Granny?"

Tod's mother looked at the handwriting. "It is," she said.

"And it's squashy like the other parcel," said Tod. "Perhaps it's another jumper with a T on it for Tod."

Tod's mother helped Tod to open the parcel and inside was another jumper. This time it was a blue jumper with a red

T for Tod knitted on the front of it. Tod was pleased. "Now I can wear this blue jumper when the red one is being washed; and I can wear the red jumper when the blue one is being washed. So I can always wear a jumper with T for Tod on the front of it!"

They telephoned Tod's granny to thank her. When Tod had thanked her, Tod's mother spoke to her: "Now you mustn't wear yourself out knitting jumpers for Tod. He has two good jumpers that will last until he grows out of them. Promise me that you won't knit Tod any more jumpers until then."

"I promise," said Tod's granny.

Then they all said goodbye to Granny – Tod said it, and Tod's mother, and Tod's teddy bear, who happened to be in the kitchen at the time.

Just about a week later, on a Friday

morning, when Tod's mother had gone off to her job and Tod's father was cooking in the kitchen, the postman called with yet another parcel for Tod. It was addressed to him in his granny's handwriting. "So perhaps it's another jumper for me after all," Tod said to his father. "Although Granny promised not to make me another jumper for ages and ages."

"And your granny never breaks her promises," said Tod's father. He was puzzled.

Between them they opened the parcel. Inside there seemed to be two jumpers, one red, one blue.

"Oh," said Tod, disappointed. "Granny's gone and knitted me just the same jumpers all over again."

Tod spread the two jumpers out on the kitchen table. Then he saw their size: they were very small – far too small for him. He cried out angrily, "These jumpers are for a tiny, tiny baby! I'm not a baby any more – I'm not!"

"Calm down, Tod," said his father. "There must be some mistake."

"No," said Tod. "She means the jumpers for me, because she's knitted big Ts on the fronts of them. Look – a blue T on the red jumper and a red T on the blue jumper. T for Tod."

Tod was almost crying, he was so furious. But his father was rummaging among the parcel-wrappings. At last he found what he was looking for: a card from Tod's granny. It had a picture of a teddy bear on the outside, and inside there was a message. When Tod's father had read the message, he began laughing. "Tod," he said, "these jumpers aren't meant for you at all."

"Don't be silly!" said Tod crossly. "Of course they are! I told you: they've got my T for Tod on their fronts."

Tod's father said, "There's somebody else in this house, much smaller than you, whose name begins with a T."

"Who?" said Tod.

"Think," said his father. "Somebody small who happens to be in the kitchen at this very moment."

Tod stood in the middle of the kitchen and turned slowly round, looking at everything as he turned, until his gaze fell upon his own teddy bear sitting on a chair.

"Oh!" he cried. "Is it Teddy?"

"Yes," said his father. "Teddy begins with a T, just as Tod does; and your granny says these jumpers should fit him nicely."

And so they did. Tod tried each one on Teddy in turn; but the jumper he decided

Tod's gaze fell upon his own teddy bear.

that Teddy must wear that day was the red one, because it was just like the one Tod was wearing.

When Tod's mother came home and saw Tod and Teddy together, she cried, "Why! You're twins – twins in the same red jumpers with blue Ts in front!"

"But my T is for Tod," Tod explained to his mother, "and Teddy's T is for Teddy." Then he told his mother about the surprise parcel from Granny.

Later, Tod telephoned his granny. He said, "This is Tod speaking, but my teddy bear wants a word with you." He held his teddy bear up to the telephone and said in a squeaky voice, "This is Teddy thanking you for his two new jumpers. Thank you. Thank you."

"What about asking your granny to come to tea tomorrow?" whispered Tod's mother.

"Yes," said Tod. Into the telephone he said, "Come to tea tomorrow, Granny, and there'll be surprises for you. Will you come to tea?"

"I'll come," said Tod's granny. "I promise."

When Tod had put the phone down, his father and mother asked what the surprises would be.

"I shall hide behind the sofa," said Tod, "and when Granny comes in, she'll say, 'Tod's not here.' And I shall jump out and say, 'Yes, he is!' And then she'll say, 'But Teddy's not here.' And I shall say, 'Yes, he is!' and I'll lift the cushion on the sofa and there he'll be. And we'll both be wearing our jumpers with Ts on the front, and Granny *will* be surprised!"

Tod was looking at the oranges.

TOD AND THE
ENORMOUS ORANGE

One afternoon Tod and his mother were in the greengrocer's. His mother was buying potatoes and cabbage. Tod was looking at the oranges: some of them were enormous. He held one of the enormous oranges up to his mother: "Can we buy this?"

"No, Tod. We've plenty of oranges at home."

"But this is an enormous orange. The oranges at home are little."

"They're oranges, Tod, and they'll do."

Tod looked very sad. "Billy brought an enormous apple to school and, at story-time, Mrs Robinson cut it up with a little knife and put all the pieces on a plate and

Billy handed the plate round and we all had a slice of his apple."

His mother said, "All right, Tod – just this once. We'll buy just one big orange for you to take to school tomorrow."

So they bought the enormous orange, and Tod carried it home in his two hands.

Tod was very, very pleased. He showed the enormous orange to his father, and explained to him about Mrs Robinson and the little knife and the plate. His father was interested, and he told Tod about where oranges come from – how, in some hot countries, oranges grow on orange trees just as apples grow on apple trees. And he told Tod that when *he* was a little boy he had saved the biggest pip from an orange he had eaten, and he had planted the pip in earth, and the pip had sprouted and grown into a little tree.

"Did it have oranges on it?" asked Tod.

"No," his father said with a sigh. "It didn't grow very tall, and it didn't live very long, and it never had any oranges on it."

"Perhaps you were unlucky," said Tod.

"Perhaps," said his father.

The next day Tod took the enormous orange to school with him. First of all he showed it to Billy, and then he played with it a little, and then he gave it to Mrs Robinson to keep until story-time.

When story-time came, all the children sat round Mrs Robinson. She had a plate and on it were the enormous orange and the little knife to peel it with. But Mrs Robinson did not begin peeling at once. She looked sadly at Tod and said, "I'm afraid your orange has been spoiled, Tod. It has a hole in it."

They all looked at the orange, and Susie said, "I can see the hole. It looks as though someone made it with their finger."

Mrs Robinson said, "Did you stick your finger into your orange, Tod?"

"No," said Tod.

"Perhaps Billy stuck a finger into your orange?" said Mrs Robinson.

"No," said Billy.

"I stuck my thumb in the orange," said Tod. "I wanted to feel if there were pips in the middle of the orange. My dad says you can grow an orange tree from an orange pip, if you're lucky."

"That's interesting," said Mrs Robinson. "But was your thumb clean, Tod?"

"I'm not sure," said Tod.

"Well," said Mrs Robinson, "I'll peel the orange and we'll see what it's like inside."

While she peeled the orange, all the children watched anxiously. Tod watched particularly anxiously.

"There!" said Mrs Robinson at last. She had peeled the orange, and they could all see that one of the pieces – but only one – was in a mess because of Tod's thumb-hole. Mrs Robinson put that piece aside with the orange peel, to be thrown away. She put all the other orange pieces out on a plate and gave Tod the plate to hand round. Billy and Susie and all the other children took a piece of orange each; and, when Tod had been round everybody, there were still three pieces left on the plate.

He offered the plate to Mrs Robinson, and she took one of the pieces. "Thank you, Tod," she said.

There were still two pieces left. "One of those is yours, anyway, Tod," said Mrs Robinson, "and I think you might as well eat the other one, too." So Tod did.

Mrs Robinson said that any children who

Mrs Robinson told them a story so interesting that Tod quite forgot the orange pips in his pocket.

had orange pips to get rid of could bring them to her. She would throw them away with the orange peel and the messed-up piece with Tod's thumb-hole in it. Billy and Susie and the rest all brought their orange pips to Mrs Robinson to be thrown away; but Tod kept his. He had two thin little pips from one orange piece and one big fat one from the other one. He put them all into his pocket for safety.

"Now for the story," said Mrs Robinson, and she told them all a story so interesting that Tod quite forgot the orange pips in his pocket.

He didn't remember the pips until his mother fetched him at the end of school and asked, "And how was the enormous orange?"

Then Tod told her about his having handed round the pieces of orange at story-time. "And, at the end," he said, "I had my piece of orange and I had an extra piece, too. And I saved my orange pips, because I'm going to plant them in our garden. I want orange trees to grow there. I want us to grow our own oranges. Lots of enormous oranges."

"Don't be disappointed, Tod," said his mother, "if the pips don't grow. But we'll try. Orange trees like to grow in hot countries, so we won't plant the pips out in the garden, where it might be too cold for them. We'll put them to grow in plant-pots indoors, where it's warmer."

At home, they chose three plant-pots from the garden shed and Tod used his trowel to fill them with earth. Then Tod's mother said, "Shall I plant the pips for you, Tod?"

"No, thank you," said Tod. "I want to

do it all by myself."

"You have to make a hole in the earth in each plant-pot," said his mother, "and then drop a pip in the hole and then fill the hole in again with earth."

"I can do all that," said Tod. "How shall I make the holes? My trowel is much too big."

"You could make the holes with your finger," said his mother, "if you didn't mind getting your finger earthy."

"I don't mind that," said Tod. "But I'd rather use my thumb. My thumb is good at making holes."

With his thumb, Tod made a hole in the earth in each of the three plant-pots and then dropped the pips in, one to each hole. Then, very gently, he trickled earth into each hole, to fill it up.

Then Tod and his mother put the three

plant-pots on the kitchen window-sill, where it was sunny. They put the plant-pot with the big fat pip in it in the middle and the plant-pots with the thin little pips on either side.

"Perhaps I'll be lucky and an orange tree will grow," said Tod.

"Perhaps," said his mother.

The first morning after planting the orange pips, Tod rushed downstairs into the kitchen to see whether any of them were growing. Nothing was growing.

The next morning Tod hurried to the kitchen again to see. Nothing again.

On the third morning there was still nothing, and Tod's father said, "You know, Tod, it may be days and days and days – it may be weeks and weeks – before an orange pip begins to grow. If one ever grows at all."

"Oh," said Tod, disappointed. Then he

cheered up. "Anyway," he said, "I can make a picture of what an orange tree will be like, when one does grow." So Tod painted a picture of a green tree growing in a reddy-brown plant-pot. The tree was hung all over with bright coloured blobs that were enormous oranges. Tod took the picture to school, and Mrs Robinson liked it so much that she stuck it up on the wall. Underneath Tod's picture she wrote for him: "This is Tod's orange tree." And she said to Tod, "Even if none of your orange pips grows, Tod, you've made a lovely picture."

"But perhaps one of my pips will grow," said Tod.

"Perhaps," said Mrs Robinson.

Nobody really thought that any of Tod's orange pips would grow. In the end, even Tod didn't think so. He forgot about the orange pips in the plant-pots on the kitchen window-sill. He didn't look there any more.

Days and days and days passed and then, one day when he was outside in the garden, he heard his mother and father calling from the house.

"Tod! Tod!" his mother called. "Come quickly, Tod!"

And his father called, "In the kitchen, Tod! Come and see!"

When Tod reached the kitchen, he saw his mother and father bent over the middle plant-pot on the kitchen window-sill. "Look!" they said. "One of your orange pips has sprouted. It's growing!"

Tod looked. He could hardly believe his eyes: an orange tree – a tiny, tiny orange tree beginning to grow in one of his plant-pots. He said, "I'll tell Mrs Robinson. I'll tell Billy. I'll tell everybody." He reached out and touched the little green shoot very carefully with one finger and said softly, "I'm very, very lucky, aren't I?"

"You are indeed," said his mother and father.

"Can't Mr Parkin take Ginger on holiday with him?" asked Tod.

TOD AND THE
DESPERATE SEARCH

The next-door neighbour, old Mr Parkin, was going away for a week's holiday. But what was going to happen to his cat, Ginger, while he was away?

"Can't Mr Parkin take Ginger on holiday with him?" asked Tod. "Wouldn't Ginger like a holiday?"

"Cats like staying at home," said Tod's mother. "Your dad and I have offered to feed Ginger while Mr Parkin's away; and Mr Parkin has said, Yes, please. He's given me his back-door key, so that we can go into the house and get the cat food every day. Ginger has half a tin of cat food every morning and another half tin every evening."

"My, that's a lot for a cat!" said Tod's father.

"Ginger's a big cat," said Tod's mother.

Tod said, "Can I come with you when you go to feed Ginger?"

"Of course," said his mother; and his father said, "You could be a great help, Tod."

So it was settled.

Ginger was a big cat, yellowy brown all over except for one white front leg. He was rather a silent cat. He never miaowed; but he purred when he was tickled behind his ear. He liked to be out of doors most of the time.

On the first morning after old Mr Parkin had gone on holiday, Tod was at home with his father. They took Mr Parkin's key and went round to the back of his house. There was Ginger at the back door, his tail waving high in the air, ready for his breakfast. They unlocked the door and went into Mr Parkin's kitchen, Ginger slipping in ahead of them. Mr Parkin had left his kitchen very neat and clean; and the door between the kitchen and the rest of the house was shut. This was so that Ginger could not go wandering off through the other rooms.

Tod's father opened a tin of cat food, while Tod washed the cat dish that Ginger had eaten his supper from the evening before. Ginger had two cat dishes to eat from, one being used, one being washed. So he always had a clean dish for his food.

Tod's father put down the clean dish with half a tin of cat food in it. Ginger began eating very fast.

While Ginger ate, Tod's father put the half used tin into the fridge; and Tod fetched Ginger's water bowl that always stood just outside the back door. He emptied the old water away and refilled the bowl with clean, fresh water from the tap and put the bowl outside again.

By now Ginger had finished his breakfast and he walked out into the garden again, very pleased with himself. He settled on the lawn in a patch of sunshine and began cleaning his fur.

"But where will he sleep tonight?" asked Tod.

"If it's cold," said Tod's father, "he can get through the cat door into the boiler-house. It's always warm in there, and Mr Parkin has put a basket there with an old blanket in it. But if the night's not cold, then Ginger will probably sleep out in the garden under a bush."

Tod's father locked Mr Parkin's back door again. They said goodbye to Ginger and went back to their own house.

That evening Tod didn't go with his mother – it was her turn – to give Ginger his supper, because he was being bathed and put to bed by his father. But every morning Tod went with his mother or his father to give Ginger his breakfast, wash a cat dish, and renew the water in the drinking bowl.

And every morning there was Ginger at Mr Parkin's back door, tail in the air, eager for his breakfast.

Then one morning, almost at the end of Mr Parkin's week away from home, Tod went as usual with his father, and Ginger was not waiting at Mr Parkin's back door.

"Bother," said Tod's father. "That cat's late for his breakfast." And he began to call him: "Ginger! Ginger!"

No Ginger came.

"You call him, Tod," said his father.

So Tod called him: "Ginger! Ginger!" and then "Ginger-ninger!" and then "Ginger-winger!"

They both called and called, but no cat came. In the end they decided to leave the dish of cat food just outside the back door, with fresh water in the drinking bowl. Perhaps Ginger would come later.

At midday Tod and his father went round to Mr Parkin's back door again. There was the dish of cat food still. It looked as if birds might have pecked at it; but most of the food remained. Ginger would have eaten the whole lot and left the dish clean. So Ginger had not been.

When Tod's mother came home, they told her about Ginger's having gone missing. "What a worry!" she said. "Mr Parkin's back the day after tomorrow. I don't know what he'll say if Ginger's not there to greet him."

*At midday Tod and his father went round
to Mr Parkin's back door again.*

"Perhaps the cat's got shut in somewhere," said Tod's father.

"Perhaps in Mr Parkin's house," said Tod.

"No," said his mother. "You remember the door from the kitchen into the rest of the house has always been kept shut. And Mr Parkin told me himself that he shut and locked every window in the house, upstairs and down, before he left."

"There's still his garden shed and his greenhouse and that boiler-house," said Tod's father. "We must search everywhere."

So all three of them went to look in Mr Parkin's garden shed and his greenhouse and the boiler-house. They even came back and looked in their own garden shed.

No Ginger anywhere.

They began to feel desperate.

Tod had never before helped to give Ginger his supper; but today, after his bath, he put on his pyjamas and his dressing-gown and his bedroom slippers and went round with his mother and his father to see if Ginger had turned up for his supper.

He hadn't.

Tod's mother said, "I hope that he hasn't strayed on to the main road and been run over by a car."

"I think Ginger's probably too sensible for that," said Tod's father.

Tod said, "I don't want Ginger to be dead."

His parents comforted him. They mustn't give up hope yet, they said. Who knows? Ginger might still turn up tomorrow.

The next morning, however, at breakfast time, outside Mr Parkin's back door, there was still no Ginger.

"I'm afraid that something must have happened to him," Tod's mother said sadly.

And Tod's father said, "Wasn't Mr Parkin going to telephone us this evening, just to confirm that he's coming home tomorrow? What on earth are we going to say to him?"

Tod's mother just said, "Oh dear!"

That morning Tod felt very miserable. His mother was at home, and she suggested various interesting things that he might like to do; but he didn't want to do any of them. He just wandered round the garden, calling, "Ginger-ninger, where are you? Ginger-winger, come home!"

Tod knew that they'd looked into their own garden shed, but he still went there again, because there seemed nowhere else he could look. The first time he looked in, he looked very quickly, because, of course, he really knew that Ginger wasn't there. The second time he decided he must look more thoroughly, all round: at the workbench under the window; at the cupboard at the far end, where his father kept his special tools; at the garden spades and forks and hoes that hung in a row along the remaining wall. Tod even got down on all fours and looked under the lawnmower. No Ginger, of course.

That was the second time that Tod looked into the shed.

The third time he looked in, he was quietly crying to himself. It was getting dark inside the shed. He looked at the cupboard at the far end. At the bottom of the cupboard, the door fitted badly and left a gap. Suddenly, through that gap, came snaking something white – a long white furry arm.

"Ginger!" shouted Tod, and rushed to open the cupboard door; but the cupboard was kept bolted, and the bolt was too high

45

for Tod to reach. So he ran back to the house to fetch his mother, who came hurrying at once. She unbolted the cupboard door and opened it – and out stalked Ginger!

Ginger didn't seem ill or even thin; but he did seem cross. He didn't want to be stroked or even tickled behind his ear. He went straight to the fence that separated the two gardens. He crouched at the bottom of the fence for a moment, and then with a leap he was at the top of the fence, and then over into his own garden – home!

Tod's mother fetched Mr Parkin's key and they went round to his back door. There was Ginger, his tail waving in the air, ready for his food. He had already had a long drink, they could tell, from his bowl of water. They fed him more than half a tin of cat food, as he had missed so many meals. Then they locked up again and went home.

Later, Tod's father heard all about how Tod had found Ginger in the tool cupboard. "What a sly cat!" he said. "Yes, I remember going to that cupboard to get a tool on the very day he disappeared. I left the cupboard door open for just a few minutes while I did something at the workbench. While my back was turned, he must have slipped in."

"Cats are like that," said Tod's mother.

"Anyway," said Tod's father, "we'll have something to tell old Parkin when he rings up."

Tod began jumping with excitement. "When Mr Parkin rings, can I tell him about Ginger? Can I? Can I?"

"Why not?" said his father, and looked at Tod's mother. She said, "I think Tod should tell the whole story. After all, he found Ginger. He is the hero of our desperate search."

"Susie's not my friend, and I don't want her
to come here and play with my toys!"

TOD AND THE VISITOR

"No, no, no!" cried Tod. "Susie's not my friend, and I don't want her to come here and play with my toys!"

"Oh, dear!" said Tod's mother. "And I've told Susie's mother that Susie can come for the whole afternoon. Susie's mother has to go and see Susie's granny, who's very ill, and there's nowhere else for Susie to go."

"I don't care," said Tod.

"Girls are nice, Tod," said Tod's father.

"And Susie's mother was so worried," said Tod's mother.

"Susie's not my friend," repeated Tod.

"But she's not your enemy?"

"No," said Tod. "But at school we don't

do things together, so she's not my friend."

"Well, Tod," said his mother, "I'm sorry, but I've promised Susie's mother, and Susie will have to come. You'll just have to be nice to her."

"No," said Tod, but he spoke very quietly, because he knew that his father and mother might get cross.

The afternoon came; and Susie came. She was just Tod's age and only a little taller. She was rather shy and quiet, because her mother had never left her at a strange house before. The only person in this house that she really knew was Tod; and she wasn't Tod's friend.

Tod's father was out at work. Tod's mother made their lunch. They had fish fingers and mashed potatoes and peas, followed by red jelly. Tod said nothing while they had lunch; and Susie said nothing. The only people who talked were Tod's mother and Susie's teddy bear, who sat up at the table with Susie. When Tod's mother asked Susie if she would like tomato ketchup with her fish fingers, Susie's teddy bear said in a squeaky voice, "Yes, please. Susie likes tomato ketchup." And when Tod's mother asked Susie if she would like a second helping of red jelly, her teddy bear squeaked again, "Yes, please. She would."

After lunch, Tod's mother said she must do the washing-up. She suggested that Tod and Susie and her teddy bear all went upstairs to Tod's room to play. Neither Tod nor Susie said anything, and Susie's teddy bear said nothing either. But Tod raced ahead upstairs to his room; Susie and her teddy bear followed very slowly.

When Susie reached Tod's room, she found him sitting on his bed with all his toys

*"You can play with anything you like except
for the things on the bed. They're mine."*

– his cars and aeroplanes and his blue rabbit and his teddy bear – everything – on the bed with him. He said, "You can play with anything you like except for the things on the bed. They're mine."

There wasn't really anything else to play with. Susie and her teddy bear went into a corner of the room and had a quiet conversation together. Once Tod heard a squeaky voice say, "I don't like it here one little bit."

After a while Susie and her teddy bear left Tod's room and went downstairs to the kitchen, where Tod's mother was finishing the washing-up. Tod heard them go into the kitchen; the door closed behind them. Then, quite soon, Tod heard the kitchen door open again, and his mother's voice, sounding very cross, called up the stairs, "Tod!"

Tod did not answer.

"Tod, can you hear me, or shall I come upstairs?"

"I can hear you," called Tod, only just loudly enough.

"Tod," called his mother, "I am NOT pleased with you!"

Then she went back into the kitchen, shutting the door behind her with quite a slam.

Tod got off his bed and put all his toys back in their proper places. He tried playing with them, but he wasn't enjoying himself much.

Then he began to notice a smell coming from downstairs, from the kitchen. It was a hot, buttery, sugary, spicy smell: most delicious. He wondered what was being cooked, and by whom. He wondered aloud to his teddy bear; and his teddy bear said in a squeaky voice, "Let's go downstairs and see."

So downstairs they went, and into the kitchen. There at the kitchen table sat Susie in a pinafore and her teddy bear with a tea towel tied round him, like another pinafore. Tod's mother said, "We've been making buns for tea. They've just gone into the oven now. There's a mixing bowl to be scraped. You and Susie could scrape the mixing bowl between you."

Susie said nothing; Tod said nothing; neither of the teddy bears spoke.

"Look," said Tod's mother, "here are two teaspoons, one for Susie and one for Tod. And look: here with my finger I'll draw a line across the inside of the mixing bowl, so that there are two halves to be scraped." Tod's mother had drawn a line with her finger, and now she licked the stickiness off her finger. "Yum, yum!" she said. "It tastes lovely! Try it."

So Susie and Tod began to scrape the bowl between them, while their two teddy bears sat up on the kitchen dresser, watching. They scraped the bowl so clean that Tod's mother said it looked as if it didn't need washing.

"Now," said Tod's mother, "while the buns are cooking, why don't you both go into the garden? There's the sandpit to play in, and the paddling pool."

"Can we take our teddies?" Susie asked.

"Of course," said Tod's mother. "But if you go paddling, don't let them get wet."

So Susie and Tod and the two teddy bears went out into the garden. First of all they went to the paddling pool. It was a proper pool, dug out of the ground. A garden gnome sat at one end of it, fishing. They sat their bears on either side of the gnome, high and dry. Susie's bear said in a squeaky voice to the gnome, "Hello, there!" And Tod's bear said in a squeaky voice, "Caught anything yet?"

The garden gnome did not answer; and Tod said, "He never speaks. My dad says it's because he's made of concrete."

After they had paddled in the paddling pool, they picked up their teddy bears and went to the sandpit. They sat on either side of the sandpit with their bare feet scuffing about in the sand.

Susie said, "I've been to the seaside, and I made sandcastles."

"So've I," said Tod. "And I buried my dad in the sand."

"Was he all right afterwards?"

"I only buried him up to his neck. He said he was quite comfortable."

"We could bury someone in the sand now," said Susie.

*"Tod! Susie! Whatever have you done
to your teddy bears?"*

"So we could," said Tod.

And they set to work.

Some time later Tod's mother came into the garden to say that tea was nearly ready. When she saw the sandpit, she cried out, "Tod! Susie! Whatever have you done to your teddy bears?" For all she could see of the two teddy bears were two heads poking up out of the sand.

"We've buried them," said Tod.

"Only up to their necks," said Susie; and her teddy bear said in a squeaky voice, "I don't mind being buried. I'm quite comfortable."

And Tod's teddy bear said, "I'm comfortable, too."

Tod's mother said, "How could you do such a thing, Tod and Susie? It'll take so long to get all the sand out of that teddy fur!"

"You told us not to let them get wet in the

paddling pool," said Tod, "and we didn't. But you didn't say we mustn't let them get sandy."

"Are you cross?" asked Susie.

"Not really," said Tod's mother. She sighed, and then she began to laugh. "What a pair you are, you two! Now you must get your bears out of the sandpit and give them a good shake to get the worst of the sand off. I'll fetch two brushes, so that you can brush out the rest."

Tod and Susie unburied their two teddies, and then they shook them, and then they brushed them. While they were brushing them, Susie's teddy cried out in a squeaky voice, "Oh, oh! It tickles!" Both teddies began laughing squeaky laughs. They laughed so much that they fell over on the grass, where they lay, still laughing.

Tod's mother came out again to say that

*Susie's teddy cried out in a squeaky voice,
"Oh, oh! It tickles!"*

tea was on the table and that Tod's father had just got home in time for it. So they went indoors and they all sat down to tea together. The buns were still warm from the oven, and Tod's father said he couldn't have made better buns himself. The two teddy bears sat on the dresser, as before, watching the tea party.

After tea, Susie's mother called for Susie and took her home. When they had gone, Tod's father said to him, "Well, you and Susie seem to be friends now."

Tod said, "We do things together, that's all."

Tod's mother asked, "Would you like Susie to come for tea again some day?"

"I don't know," said Tod.

"Does your teddy bear know?" asked Tod's mother.

Tod's teddy bear began jumping with

excitement. He called out in a squeaky voice, "Let's have Susie's teddy to tea again! I like Susie's teddy bear! He's my friend!"

"Well," said Tod's mother. "We can't ask Susie's teddy without asking Susie as well."

"I suppose not," said Tod. "So we'll ask them both to come. My teddy would like that."

*Tod was in the bath and his father
was washing his back for him.*

TOD AND THE
BIRTHDAY PRESENT

Tod had had a birthday, with birthday cards and birthday presents, and a party with a birthday cake with candles, and party games afterwards.

"What a birthday!" said his father at the end of the day. He was putting Tod to bed, while Tod's mother finished the clearing up downstairs. Tod was in the bath and his father was washing his back for him. "And remember, Tod," said his father, "another birthday very soon!"

"No," said Tod. "I only have one birthday a year, that's all. I know that; and you're just being silly."

"Not your birthday," his father said. "It's

your mum who'll be having the birthday."

"Oh," said Tod. He took the sponge from his father and washed his knees while he thought. "Are you giving her a birthday present?"

"Of course," said his father. "I've bought it already. It's a silk scarf of the colours she likes. There's a lot of blue in it to go with the colour of her eyes."

"Is Granny giving her a present?"

"Yes, a pair of warm gloves."

Tod stood up in the bath. He was quite clean by now. He said, "I want to give her something special. I'll buy her that helicopter in the toy shop window."

"Do you think she'd really like that?"

"I would. That helicopter would be my best thing."

"She's different, Tod."

Tod thought, while his father towelled him

dry. "All right, then. Not the helicopter," he said. "But I want to give her something really, really special. I'll have to think."

"You do that," said his father. "And remember, Tod: most of all she'd like to be given something you've made for her."

"I'll remember," said Tod.

All the next day, on and off, Tod thought, and then he asked his father, "Could you teach me how to knit?"

"I think so," said his father. "But why?"

"I could knit something for her birthday present. A little mat in blue wool, to go with the colour of her eyes."

So Tod's father looked out some blue wool in the wool bag, and a pair of knitting-needles, and he began to teach Tod to knit. It was very difficult. In the middle of Tod's lesson, his mother walked into the room. She asked at once, "What are you two doing with my knitting-needles? And isn't that my wool?"

"Yes," said Tod's father. "But it's all right. I'm just teaching Tod to knit. He needs to knit something special."

At that Tod threw the knitting-needles and the wool down on the floor and shouted at his father, "Now you've spoilt everything! It won't be a surprise!"

His father began to apologize; and his mother said quickly, "Tod, I didn't see properly what you were doing, and I didn't hear properly what was said. I don't know anything."

"Yes, you do," said Tod. "You're just pretending not to know. But I know you know, and you know I know you know. And it's all ruined!"

Tod burst into tears and rushed out of the house and into the garden. He rushed down

*Tod threw the knitting-needles and
the wool down on the floor.*

to the very bottom of the garden, behind the garden shed, where he often went when he was feeling upset or miserable.

He was a long time coming back, but his father waited for him. At last he appeared, walking quite briskly and looking rather pleased with himself. He said, "I found something special down at the bottom of the garden."

"You've not been in my shed?" said his father.

"No," said Tod. "I was just looking down, feeling cross, when I saw something lying on the earth where you'd been digging."

"Well, what was it?"

"It's in my pocket," said Tod, "and I'm not going to tell you what it is or what I'm going to make with it, because you can't keep a secret. It's going to be my surprise for the birthday."

Tod went upstairs into the bathroom and shut the door. Then Tod's father heard him washing something in the wash-basin. He scrubbed something with the nail-brush, and then he dried something on the bath towel. Then he came out of the bathroom and went into his own bedroom and hid something there.

Then Tod came downstairs and said to his father, "I'll need string."

"There's a ball of string in the kitchen drawer," said his father.

"No," said Tod. "Not ordinary string. Pretty string. Blue string."

"I think we may have to buy some specially in a shop," said Tod's father.

"I have money," said Tod.

The next Saturday Tod and his father went shopping in the nicest shop in town. Tod's father said to the shop lady, "We want to buy some specially pretty string."

"Blue," said Tod.

"I could perhaps be of more assistance," said the shop lady, "if I knew what the string was needed for."

"You'd better have a private talk with my son about that," said Tod's father. "I'll be at the men's socks counter."

Tod's father went quite a long way off to the men's socks counter. Tod could see him there, and he could see Tod, but he was too far off to hear what Tod was saying.

Tod said to the shop lady, "I'm making a birthday present for my mum. It's to be a surprise, so it has to be kept a secret from my dad, because he's such a chatterbox." Tod looked over at his father; but his father was looking at men's socks. Tod brought something out of his pocket and showed it to the shop lady.

*Tod brought something out of his pocket
and showed it to the shop lady.*

"Aha!" said she. "Now I understand why you were thinking of pretty string. But wouldn't ribbon be better – narrow velvet ribbon in a pretty colour?"

"Blue," said Tod, "because her eyes are blue. And velvet ribbon would be good."

So the shop lady got out a drawer full of velvet ribbons of different widths and colours. Tod chose the narrowest ribbon of a beautiful blue, and the shop lady advised him of the length he would need. She cut off that length and parcelled it up for him, and he paid for it. Then he went off to the men's socks counter and told his father that he was ready to go home.

On the way home, Tod said, "All I need now is an empty matchbox for my present to go into."

"Will it be small enough for a matchbox?" Tod's father asked in astonishment.

"I've just said," said Tod.

When they got home, Tod's father couldn't find an empty matchbox, but he did find two boxes only partly full of matches. Tod saw what must be done. He emptied all the matches from one box into the other, so that one box was full of matches and the other was quite empty. In the middle of his doing this, Tod's mother walked in. "Whatever are you two doing with the matches?" she asked.

"Just rearranging them in their boxes," said Tod's father; and Tod quietly said to him, "Well done!"

Tod's mother didn't ask any more questions.

That evening Tod stuck white paper all over the empty matchbox. Then he decorated it with pink and blue crayons. He drew a little picture of himself on top with a balloon coming out of his mouth. Inside the balloon he got his father to write:

HAPPY BIRTHDAY!

The next day was the birthday. Everyone was ready for it, and Tod's granny came for the whole day and to spend the night.

At breakfast time, Tod's mother's birthday presents were arranged round her plate. First of all she opened the parcel that had the silk scarf in it. "It's just what I wanted!" she said to Tod's father. "Thank you!"

Then she opened Tod's granny's parcel with the warm gloves inside. "Just what I wanted!" she said to Tod's granny. "Thank you!"

Then she came to the matchbox. "Whatever is this?" she wondered; and Tod's father and his granny both said, "Whatever is it?"

Tod's mother came to the matchbox.
"Whatever is this?"

Tod's mother opened the matchbox. "Oh!" she cried in amazement. She lifted out of the matchbox a narrow blue velvet ribbon with its two ends tied firmly together. Dangling from the ribbon was a small, unusual-shaped stone. The stone was a pretty, light brown with white markings. What made the stone so unusual was a hole that went right through the middle of it. The blue velvet ribbon went through that hole.

"Oh!" said Tod's mother again. "It's to hang round my neck." And she hung it round her neck. "It's a pendant."

"Yes," said Tod. "That's exactly what it is. Not a necklace; a pendant. That's what the shop lady said it would be."

"It's so pretty!" said Tod's mother. "The velvet ribbon – "

"Blue," said Tod. "To go with the colour of your eyes."

" – And the stone is so pretty and so very, very unusual, with a hole right through the middle of it. Wherever did you find such a stone, Tod?"

"Just in the garden," said Tod. "I wasn't even looking for it. But, as soon as I saw it, I thought I could make something really special for your birthday."

"And so you did!" said his mother. "Thank you, Tod! Thank you!"

Tod's mother wore her pendant all day. In the evening, Tod's father was going to take her out for a birthday treat; and, while they were out, Tod's granny would look after him.

Tod was in bed and his granny was just going to read him his bedtime story, when Tod's mother came in to say good-night. She was already dressed for going out; she had her coat on, and her birthday scarf and her birthday gloves. As she bent over to kiss Tod, something swung forward from between the folds of the scarf and knocked gently against Tod's face: the pendant. Tod put up his hand and took the brown and white stone between his fingers.

"Do you really like it?" he asked.

"Very, very much."

"But you never said it was just what you wanted."

"How could I, Tod? I couldn't have wanted such a thing, because I couldn't possibly have imagined that such a thing existed: a beautiful stone with a hole through it, found in our very own garden and made by you into a pendant, just for me! It still amazes me, and it's one of the loveliest presents I've ever had."

"Good," said Tod.

When Tod heard the front door close

behind his mother and father, he said to his granny, "She's having a specially nice birthday, isn't she? And now you can start reading to me, please."

Tod said, "I think I'll do an exploration."

TOD AND THE WILDEST
COUNTRY IN THE WORLD

One sunny Saturday afternoon Tod said, "I think I'll do an exploration."

"Where?" said his mother.

"Just down the garden," said Tod.

"You do that," said his father. "We'll finish the washing-up."

"I'll need provisions, of course," said Tod.

So his mother put some peanuts and raisins in a little bag and put the bag in Tod's trouser pocket. "And you can eat a few raspberries as you go," she said.

"And what about water?" asked his father.

"No," said Tod. "Explorers drink from

the lakes and rivers they cross. But I shall need my gun."

"Surely you're not going to shoot anyone!" cried his mother.

"Of course not," said Tod. "And anyway, there won't be any people. Where I'm going is uninhabited. It's the wildest country in the world. But there might be wild animals, and they might attack me."

Tod fetched his wooden gun. "I wish I could sling it over my shoulder," he said. "You see, I'll need my hands free to climb mountains."

"Wait!" said his father. He took off his belt and fixed it to the gun in a loop. "There!" he said.

"Well done!" said Tod. "Thank you." And he slung the gun over his shoulder. "There's just one more thing," he said. "I need something to look through. I mean, so that I can see far into the distance."

"You're not having my binoculars," said his father.

"They'd be good," said Tod. "They're hanging in their case on the back of your bedroom door."

"No!" said his father. "Who lost my penknife?"

"As a matter of fact," said Tod's mother. "I think you did. Through that hole in your pocket. When you were mowing the lawn."

"That's as may be," said Tod's father. "But I'm not lending him my binoculars."

Tod sighed.

"I tell you what, Tod," said his mother. "Why not take a telescope – a spyglass that you put up just to one eye? Sailors used to use them all the time."

"Have you got a telescope?" asked Tod.

"I can make one in a twink," said his

"I'll be back for tea," said Tod.

mother. She unwound the last of the kitchen paper from the kitchen roll. Inside the kitchen roll was a long cardboard tube. "There!" said Tod's mother.

Tod put the tube to his eye and looked through it. "Yes," he said, "this will be good. I wish it had a case with a strap to carry it by. The binoculars have a case with a strap."

"I've an idea," said Tod's father. "Look! Your telescope would fit perfectly over the barrel of your gun."

And so it did.

"Now you're ready," said Tod's mother and father. "Provisions. Gun. Telescope. Off you go."

"I'll be back for tea," said Tod.

"Keep a watch out for my penknife!" Tod's father called after him.

The first bit of exploration was not hard

going: Tod walked across the garden lawn. Then came the rockery; and the rockery was piled quite high with sharp, difficult rocks on it. Tod was glad that his hands were free for the climbing.

When Tod reached the top of the rocky mountain range, he was quite puffed. He sat down on the topmost rock, facing the way he had come, and put his telescope to his eye. He could see his home quite clearly. He could see his mother and father standing at the kitchen window, doing the washing-up. They waved at him; he waved back.

Then Tod rose to his feet and began the descent on the far side of the rocky range. He saw his home no longer.

Now Tod came to a jungle of currant bushes and raspberry-canes. He stopped in the jungle to eat raspberries – just a few. They were very refreshing.

He came out of the jungle and saw before him a wide water. At one end of it a gnome sat on a toadstool, fishing. Tod asked him, "Please, is this water dangerously deep?"

There was no answer.

"Are there crocodiles?"

Still no answer.

"Anyway," said Tod, "a crocodile hasn't come out of the water to eat you, which would be very easy. So there can't be any crocodiles to speak of. I'll risk it."

He held his gun high over his head to keep it dry, and stepped into the water. As he waded, the water got deeper; but luckily it never got deep enough to bother him. He clambered safely out on to the far bank. The bottoms of his trousers were wet, but the sun was hot and began drying them at once.

The sun was so hot as he was crossing the sandpit, that he began to worry about sunstroke in the middle of the desert. Just then he saw ahead of him a great clump of rhubarb. Thankfully he went up to it and pulled the biggest stick of rhubarb that he could see. He held it up by its stalk and its huge leaf made a sunshade over his head.

He went on. Now he was among the cabbages and cauliflowers, the peas and beans and spinach. Suddenly – what was that?

Ahead of him something was moving stealthily among the vegetable plants. Tod stopped dead. He held his breath.

Yes, some creature that was yellowish – gingery – was on the move ahead of him.

Very quietly he laid aside his sunshade and unslung his gun. He took the telescope off the barrel of his gun and laid it beside the sunshade. He levelled the gun, but he would not fire except in self-defence.

The tigerish shape did not attack him. It slunk to the fence, paused, and then with one splendid leap was up and then over.

"One of the big cats for sure!" said Tod, beginning to breathe again as usual. He replaced the telescope on the gun and slung the gun over his shoulder and picked up his sunshade and went on.

But now he was tired, and hungry, too. Just past the garden shed, he came to a hillock of grass – of cut grass. He climbed on to it, and lay down. He took his bag of provisions out of his pocket. He took out a peanut and ate it. He took out a raisin and ate it. He ate another peanut; he ate another raisin. Another peanut; another raisin. Peanut; raisin. Peanut; raisin. Peanut; raisin...

When he had eaten the last peanut and the last raisin, he closed his eyes and fell fast asleep.

"I want my tea!"

"Tod! Tod!" came his father's voice calling. It was teatime, and his father had come to find him. He woke Tod, and said, "Tod, I presume!"

Tod said, "Don't be silly!" He had woken up cross, and there was something underneath him in the grass clippings, something small and hard and knobbly, that was hurting him. He felt underneath himself and brought the thing out.

"Why, Tod, you've found my penknife!" cried his father. "I must have dropped it, after all, when I was mowing the lawn. Thank you, Tod, thank you!" He put the penknife safely into a pocket without a hole in it.

Tod felt less cross now, but he said, "I want my tea."

"At once!" said Tod's father. He swung Tod up on his shoulders and started back at a gallop up the garden – past the garden shed – through the cabbages and cauliflowers and peas and beans and spinach – past the rhubarb – across the sandpit – splashing through the ornamental paddling pool ("Sorry!" he called to the gnome as he drenched him in water) – through the currant bushes and raspberry-canes – and with one great leap right over the rockery ("Whoops!" shouted Tod) they were on the lawn.

And there was tea waiting for them, with two visitors: Tod's granny, just arrived; and Mr Parkin's cat, Ginger, from next door, with his tail waving high in the air, hopeful of a saucer of milk. There was milk for Ginger; and for the others a pot of tea and a big plate of scones, fresh baked by Tod's father, and raspberry jam to go with them.

While they had tea, Tod's mother and his

granny asked him all about his exploration and how he had come to find his father's penknife.

Then Tod's granny asked him, "Will you go exploring again tomorrow, Tod?"

"No," said Tod. "I've done that. Tomorrow I think I'll go into space."